Hello, Family Members,

Learning to read is one of the most impo... W9-BYG-879
of early childhood. **Hello Reader!** books are designed to help
children become skilled readers who like to read. Beginning
readers learn to read by remembering frequently used words
like "the," "is," and "and"; by using phonics skills to decode new
words; and by interpreting picture and text clues. These books
provide both the stories children enjoy and the structure they
need to read fluently and independently. Here are suggestions
for helping your child.

- Have your child think about a word he or she does not
  recognize right away. Provide hints such as "Let's see if we
  know the sounds" and "Have we read other words like this
  one?"
- Encourage your child to use phonics skills to sound out new
  words.
- Provide the word for your child when more assistance is
  needed so that he or she does not struggle and the experi-
  ence of reading with you is a positive one.
- Encourage your child to have fun by reading with a lot of
  expression . . . like an actor!

I do hope that you and your child enjoy this book.

>—Francie Alexander
>Reading Specialist,
>Scholastic's Learning Ventures

Activity Pages

In the back of the book are skill-building activities. These are designed to
give children further reading and comprehension practice and to provide
added enjoyment. Offer help with directions as needed and encourage
your child to have FUN with each activity.

Game Cards

In the middle of the book are eight pairs of game cards. These are designed
to help your child become more familiar with words in the book and to
play fun games.

- Have your child use the word cards to find matching words in the story.
Then have him or her use the picture cards to find matching words in the
story.
- Play a matching game. Here's how: Place the cards face up. Have your
child match words to pictures. Once the child feels confident matching
words to pictures, put cards face down. Have the child lift one card, then
lift a second card to see if both match. If the cards match, the child can
keep them. If not, place the cards face down once again.
Keep going until he or she finds all matches.

For Brian, pumpkin pie baker extraordinaire
—J.E.G.

For my grandfather (Pap)
who first showed me the joys of gardening.
—T.S-L.

ISBN: 0-439-20056-3

Text copyright © 2000 by Jane E. Gerver.
Illustrations copyright © 2000 by Tammie Speer-Lyon.
All rights reserved. Published by Scholastic Inc.
SCHOLASTIC, HELLO READER, CARTWHEEL BOOKS and associated logos are trademarks and/or registered trademarks of Scholastic Inc.

Library of Congress Cataloging-in-Publication Data

Gerver, Jane E.
    Grow a pumpkin pie! / by Jane E. Gerver; illustrated by Tammie Speer-Lyon.
        p. cm. — (My first hello reader!)
    Summary: Describes the process of making a pumpkin pie, from planting the seed, through caring for the plant, to cooking the pie.
        ISBN 0-439-20056-3 (pb)
        1. Pumpkin—Juvenile literature. 2. Cookery (Pumpkin)—Juvenile literature. [1. Pumpkin. 2. Cookery—Pumpkin.] I. Lyon, Tammie, ill. II. Title. III. Series.
SB347 .G47 2000   99-087748
635'.62—dc21   CIP

10 9 8 7 6 5 4 3 2   01 02 03 04

Printed in the U.S.A.   24
First printing, September 2000

Grow a Pumpkin Pie!

by Jane E. Gerver
Illustrated by Tammie Speer-Lyon

My First Hello Reader!
With Game Cards

SCHOLASTIC INC.

New York   Toronto   London   Auckland   Sydney
Mexico City   New Delhi   Hong Kong

Dig a hole.

Plant a seed.

Water well.

Pull a weed.

Here comes rain.

Splash in mud!

Shoots come up.

Then a bud.

Look! We see

a long green vine.

Little pumpkins grow

in a line.

The air gets cold.

Leaves fall down—

orange, yellow,

red, and brown.

Pumpkins ripen

on the ground.

Pick one that is
big and round.

Cut the top.

Start to scoop.

Add eggs and cream.

It looks like soup.

Stir in sugar

with your spoon.

Hurry, hurry!

It's almost noon!

Mix in spices.

Let's be quick!

Stir some more.

Now it's thick.

Pour it in
a crusty shell.
Place in the oven.
Bake it well.

It must cool.

Let it sit.

Take a fork.

Taste a bit.

Don't forget

to save a seed.

Plant it next year—

it's all you need!

seeds

What Comes First?

What comes first? What comes second?
What comes third? What comes last?

Match the Pumpkins

Which pumpkins are small? Which ones are tall? Which ones are round? Which ones are lumpy and bumpy?

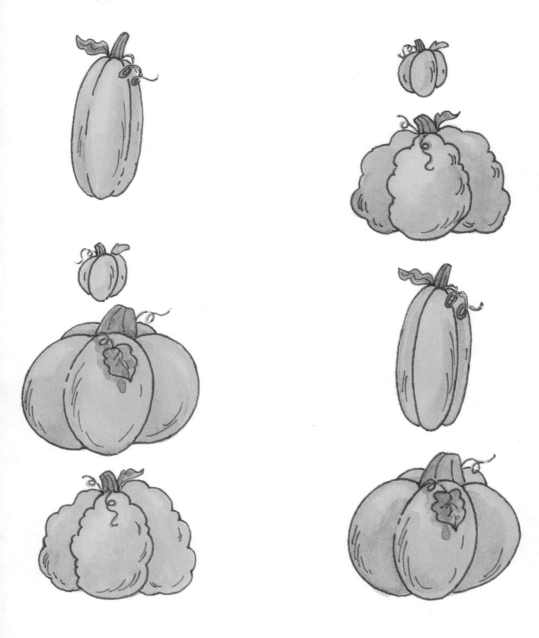

Pumpkin Patch Maze

Find the way through the maze. Start at the gate. End at the pumpkin patch. Don't cross any lines along the way!

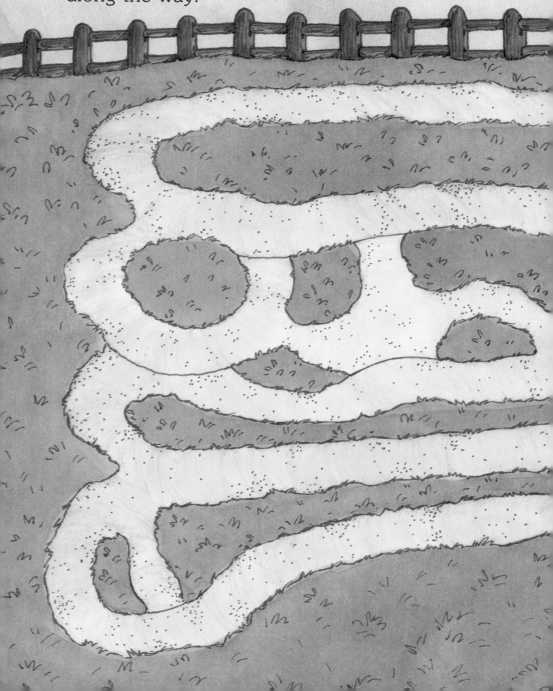

Start

Finish

Rhyme Time

Match the word to the picture it rhymes with.

dig

line

noon

weed

Pumpkin Faces

Draw a face on this pumpkin with a crayon
or a pencil. Is your pumpkin happy or sad?
Is your pumpkin awake or sleepy?

What Comes First?

first second third fourth

Pumpkin Patch Maze

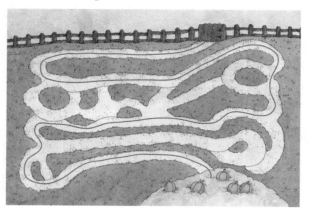

Match the Pumpkins

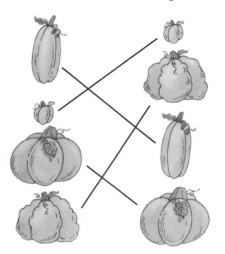

Rhyme Time

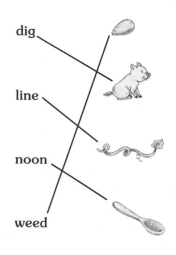

dig

line

noon

weed